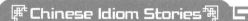

U0109062

THE MAGIC FOUR

1

Written by Catherine Chan & Simon Lau
Illustrated by William Ma

Preface

You may be wondering why this book is titled *The Magic Four...*

The magic is that with just four Chinese characters, you can take a wide peek into the rich history and culture of China.

Chinese idioms, or Chengyu, are like little time capsules - each one of these 20 idioms carries stories of former dynasties, from intrigue and mind games in the royal court, to generals strategising on the battlefield, to glimpses of daily life in ancient China.

This volume – the first one in a set of three – is based on animals. The idioms include a mantis who thinks it is strong that it can stop a carriage; a farmer who thinks he can just wait for a rabbit to crash into a tree so he can take one home for dinner every night; and even mythical creatures such as the dragon who unexpectedly pays its superfan a visit only to be disappointed.

Not only does the book have the literal meaning of each Chinese idioms, it also shows what the idioms actually mean today. A similar idiom in the English language is provided with an example of its use; in addition, four extra English words and two English idioms/phrases used in each story are explained, and sentences examples of idioms/phrases are given to show how they are used in the correct context.

Reading these stories will help you gain a greater appreciation of Chinese wisdom accumulated over thousands of years. So, turn the page and get ready to be enchanted by *The Magic Four*!

Catherine Chan, Simon Lau & William Ma

Contents

投 鼠 忌 器
Don't rock the boat

Jia Yi, an upright politician who lived during the time of the Western Han Dynasty, could feel his heart thump as loud as a drum during Lunar New Year celebrations. He was waiting to see the king about a matter that had troubled him for some time.

Jia Yi was opposed to his majesty being influenced by **corrupt** officials. Other officials who were loyal to the king also shared the same concern but could not decide on how to confront their leader as they were worried he might become **furious**.

They **dithered** over the issue for so long that they eventually kept their mouths shut. Jia Yi, though, was not going to **play it safe**.

When the doors finally opened, he entered the court and stood before the king.

"Your Majesty," Jia Yi said, "I wish to inform you of people who harm our kingdom, but first let me share with you a tale called 'The rat and the vase'."

"Hmm," the king murmured, "you've intrigued me. Go ahead."

Jia Yi continued: "An antiques lover has a huge collection of valuable furniture and vases in his home. One day, a rat enters his home and scurries all over the room. The antiques collector is so annoyed when the rat stops in front of a precious vase."

The king was eager to hear the rest of the story. He asked: "And what did the collector do?"

"He quietly picked up a stone to throw at the rat but then stopped himself," came the reply.

"Why did he do that?" The king asked. "I hate rats. I would have smashed the little bugger without hesitation."

"Your Majesty, the collector faced a **dilemma**. He wanted to kill the rat but at the same time feared breaking his vase with his stone."

"What a tough decision to make!" said the king.

Jia Yi seized the moment to hammer the point home: "Your Majesty, the upright officials in our court face a similar problem and cannot decide what to do.

"Just like the collector was afraid of damaging his vase if he threw the stone, your loyal officials fear damaging the trust you have bestowed onto them if they reveal the corrupters."

The king then understood his advisers were in a tricky position. He now knew what to do.

Literal meaning

avoid hitting the rat for fear of breaking the vase

Figurative meaning

being hesitant to take action or make a decisive move because something bad might happen as a result

Similar phrase in English

not wanting to rock the boat

e.g. Katie is so happy. I **don't want to rock the boat** by telling her that her husband made a mess in the kitchen.

Learn about words

1. **corrupt** adj. : dishonest and using your position for personal gain
2. **furious** adj. : very angry
3. **dither** v. : to be unable to make a decision
4. **dilemma** n. : a difficult choice between two things

Learn some phrases

1. play safe

   to not take risks

   e.g. That looks like rat meat. **Play it safe** and eat vegetables instead.

2. hammer home

   to make something understood by expressing it very clearly

   e.g. Grandpa Joe took out his false teeth to **hammer home** the importance of brushing your teeth.

對 牛 彈 琴
Cast pearls before swine

"Bravo! Bravo! We want more!" Gongming Yi was at home and enjoying the memory of his zither performance the night before, and how his adoring fans screamed for more music. He was **gratified** at the audience members crying bucket-loads of tears because they were so moved by his zither playing skills.

"Beyond a shadow of a doubt, I am the greatest ever zither player!" he thought, feeling smug. "Who cannot be touched by such sweet-sounding music that speaks to the soul?"

He looked at the field outside his home and saw an ox chewing the cud while swishing its tail under fluffy clouds drifting slowly by. Gongming Yi felt inspired.

"Some music is needed to make that ox appreciate the beauty of its environment!" he cried. He grabbed his zither and ran across the field. He sat near the ox and played his instrument with his eyes closed.

"Ah! This music is divine... truly sublime!" he thought. He was sure it could turn a violent criminal into a blubbering baby.

He opened his eyes, expecting to see the ox crying a river. But this beast only chewed the grass like before.

Gongming Yi decided to play another piece that he felt would surely turn that ox into an emotional mess. He **plucked** the strings to create even more melodious sounds, putting his heart and soul into playing it well. This was music for the gods, he thought.

He opened his right eye to peek at the ox. He expected this bovine creature to be on its knees, feeling **humble** to be in the presence of such greatness. But no, it did not.

Gongming Yi could not believe it. Was the animal deaf? After all, there was nothing wrong with his music... or was there? He decided to test the ox: he made a low, buzzing sound by continually plucking one string of his zither.

This time the cow pricked its ears. Swish, swish. Its tail moved from side to side, trying to **swat** imaginary flies that it thought were buzzing around its bottom.

The zither player finally had his eyes opened and sighed. "I overestimated this simple creature, who can neither understand nor appreciate great music."

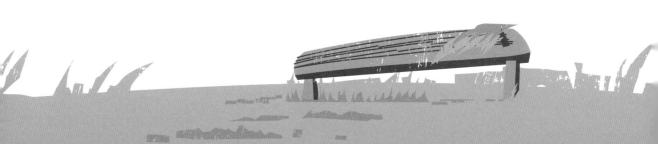

Literal meaning

to play the Chinese zither to an ox

Figurative meaning

offering something to an unappreciative audience

Similar phrase in English

cast pearls before swine

> e.g. I am **casting pearls before swine**. It was wrong to teach these ignorant people about how amazing Mozart's music is.

Learn about words

1. gratify **v.** : to make someone feel happy
2. pluck **v.** : to play a music instrument by pulling up a string
3. humble **adj.** : feeling not important
4. swat **v.** : to hit something, especially insects

Learn some phrases

1. beyond a shadow of a doubt

   feeling certain something is absolutely true

   > e.g. It is clear **beyond a shadow of a doubt** that Mary ate my doughnut after seeing her lips were covered with sugar.

2. heart and soul

   all of one's energy and passion

   > e.g. I put my **heart and soul** into writing this poem about my trousers.

狐假虎威
The cunning fox's tiger power

King Xuan, the ruler of Chu during the Warring States Period, was at the royal court and surrounded by his ministers. He had a **puzzled** look on his face.

"Why on Earth are the northern kingdoms afraid of General Zhao Xixu?" he asked his trusted advisers. "Do they fear him because of his mighty reputation?"

It was so quiet that a silent fart could have been heard if someone dared to let one out. But one minister did speak up.

"Your Highness, let me tell you a story," the minister Jiang Yi said. "In a forest, a hungry tiger was hunting for food. He spotted a fox hiding under a bush. **In a flash**, he **pounced** on the fox.

"The tiger held the fox tightly in his paw and licked his lips. Suddenly the fox cried out: 'Stop! How dare you eat me! Don't you know who I am?'

"The tiger was startled at how fearlessly and impudently the fox spoke to him. The fox was actually scared witless but had nothing to lose so he continued:

"'You obviously don't, you ignorant fool! The Heavenly Emperor appointed me the king of the beasts. If you eat me, the Emperor will give such brutal punishment that you will be begging for mercy. Is that what you want?' The fox felt encouraged to go further when he sensed some fear and doubt in the tiger's eyes.

"'If you don't believe me,' the fox said, 'walk behind

me and see how the animals react when they see me.' The tiger let go of the fox. He followed the fox, who held his head up high while taking big strides.

"The tiger quickly noticed a pattern: small animals they encountered would freeze in terror and then flee. Every time this happened, the tiger's steps became increasingly light, **timid**, and shaky. After a leopard, the tenth animal they saw, ran away at top speed, the fox, with a **manic** look on his face, turned around and started walking towards the tiger. The once fearless tiger began to walk backwards.

"'So, do you want me to tell the Emperor that you tried to eat me?' the fox teased. 'If not, get lost and don't let me see you again!' Now it was the turn of the tiger to flee as if his life depended on it.

"The tiger mistakenly believed the fox made animals flee, but they were actually afraid of the tiger himself. The cunning fox had merely used the tiger's presence and powerful reputation to intimate the creatures. In the same way, the people of the northern kingdoms are not afraid of Zhao Xixu but are terrified of the one-million-strong army behind him."

King Xuan smiled. He now understood that his enemies were afraid of his power and authority.

Literal meaning

the fox borrows the tiger's power

Figurative meaning

to use the power of strong people to bully others

Similar phrase in English

to trade on

e.g. Billy **traded on** his younger brother's fear of their mum to make him clean their bedroom and go to bed early.

Learn about words

1. **puzzled** adj. : confused from not understanding something

2. **pounce** v. : to jump onto something quickly to catch it

3. **timid** adj. : shy and having no confidence

4. **manic** adj. : describes someone's expression as being strange or crazy

Learn some phrases

1. in a flash

very quickly or suddenly

e.g. **In a flash**, David hid his phone under the blanket and took out his textbooks just before his dad entered his bedroom.

2. scared witless

extremely frightened

e.g. I was **scared witless** when I saw cockroaches coming out from Ben's house.

守株待兔
No such thing as a free lunch

Frankie the farmer was out in his field. He shivered on that cold spring morning while digging up the soil. It was tiring work, he hated waking up at 4 am every morning and he had to wait months for his crops to grow.

"A farmer's life is so hard," he thought.

"Woof, woof, woof!"

Frankie stopped thinking to himself and turned around to see a wild dog chasing a terrified, white rabbit. The little furry creature **zipped** about, trying to escape from the **rabid** dog. The rabbit then turned its head to look behind and see how close that canine was.

BANG! The poor creature had run up against a tree. It bumped its head against the trunk so hard that it was as dead as a dodo. Frankie ran over to where it lay.

"Get out of here! Shoo! Shoo!" Frankie swung his hoe at the dog until the animal retreated. Frankie then picked up the rabbit and went home. He could not believe his luck.

"Hey, Woman!" the farmer said to his wife when he arrived home.

"Don't you 'Hey Woman' me!" his wife spat back. "And why are you back so early? I can't believe I married such a bone-idle, work-shy, good-for-nothing layabout."

Frankie flung the dead rabbit at her and put his feet up on the table. For the first time since the day he got married, he felt like a real man.

"Stop your **nagging** and start cooking. Make us a delicious rabbit stew!"

After Frankie finished his tasty meal, he decided he would never farm the land ever again and instead make money the quick and easy way. Every day, he sat by the tree in his field, expecting rabbits to crash into the tree. But he would go home at the end of each day **empty-handed** only to be nagged by his wife.

"Be a real man and grow some crops to sell! I should have listened to my mother years ago when she told me not to get married to you."

"My luck will change soon," Frankie grumbled, "and I'll be bringing three rabbits home every evening!"

Months later, two villagers passed by Frankie's field. He was still sitting by that tree with a wide-eyed stare and mumbling some words to himself.

"Frankie the Fool is still waiting for a rabbit," the villager said while shaking his head.

"He has no choice but to wait for one now," his friend said. "He hasn't taken care of his field for a long time and now it's barren. There's no way he can grow crops there anymore."

Literal meaning

waiting by a tree trunk for rabbits

Figurative meaning

describes someone who prefers to sit back and wait for opportunities

Similar phrase in English

no such thing as a free lunch

e.g. Don't accept that expensive handbag from that man who wants to marry you. There's **no such thing as a free lunch**!

Learn about words

1. zip v. : move around quickly

2. rabid adj. : describes a mad animal infected by rabies

3. nagging n. : complaining or criticising

4. empty-handed adj. : not bringing or taking something

Learn some phrases

1. as dead as a dodo

something is dead for certain

e.g. That cockroach under my foot is **as dead as a dodo**.

2. have no choice but to do something

to have to do something because it is impossible to do anything else

e.g. Poor Ray kept sneezing after petting that cat. He **had no choice but to** stay away from it.

葉公好龍
Talk the talk, but not walk the walk

Eva, the town's seamstress, was in the main hall of Lord Ye's palace to present 100 underpants for her lord's inspection. She had spent all week embroidering different designs of dragons on the front of the underpants.

"Ooh, that's lovely!" he squealed with delight.

Lord Ye was a man who loved dragons. He loved the way they looked. He loved how powerful they were. He loved how they could summon wind and rain and fly high in the sky. He loved dragons so much that he would think about them all day and all night.

And how did he show his love for them? By having their image everywhere in his palace. He had them painted all over the walls of his home so that visitors always saw one whichever way they looked. He had dragons **carved** on chairs, on beds, on the ceiling, and on **pillars**.

Everything he wore had this **mythical** beast on it. He would be tucked up in bed wearing pyjamas that had dragons all over them. He padded around his palace wearing slippers that had this great creature's image sewn on the front.

Up in heaven, the dragon king heard about Lord Ye's obsession. It was flattered that a human loved its kind instead of fearing them.

"What a **splendid** fellow!" it said. "I must pay this Lord Ye a visit. He would be so happy to see me."

Thunder and lightning filled the sky as the dragon king swooped down to Earth.

BOOM!

It landed with such a heavy thud in front of Lord Ye's home that everything shook like an earthquake happened. Its long tail pushed through the front doors of the main hall where Lord Ye was. The dragon king smashed a window at the back of the hall when it **poked** its head through.

"Surprise! It's me!" it said. Lord Ye froze when the dragon's head was a few inches away from his own.

"AIYEEE!" Lord Ye went through the back door faster than cockroaches scuttling away when the lights are turned on. He ran out of his palace while screaming his head off.

"Oh dear!" the dragon king said. "What Lord Ye loves are not real dragons... only things that look like us."

Literal meaning

Lord Ye loves dragons

Figurative meaning

pretending to like something when you actually don't

Similar phrase in English

talk the talk, but not walk the walk

e.g. Bobby said he can eat 50 eggs in five minutes but I doubt that. He **talks the talk but cannot walk the walk**.

Learn about words

1. **carve** v. : to make something by cutting into something

2. **pillar** n. : a strong column that supports a building

3. **mythical** adj. : existing only in ancient myths

4. **splendid** adj. : excellent

Learn some phrases

1. **pay someone a visit**

   to visit someone

   e.g. I am happy to know that my friend who lives overseas is going to **pay me a visit**.

2. **scream one's head off**

   to scream very loudly

   e.g. Andrew **screamed his head off** while riding the rollercoaster.

畫 龍 點 睛
The final touch

"What a joke! Are you drunk today?" That was what a bystander said to the famous painter Zhang Sengyou after the latter replied to a query about his new wall painting.

The crowd that had gathered around the walls of Anle Temple in Jinling for three days were laughing so hard at Zhang Sengyou's reply that they nearly peed themselves. On those walls, the freshly painted images of four dragons were so vivid and lifelike that they almost seemed real.

"I am not joking and I am not drunk," Zhang Sengyou said. "What I just said is entirely correct."

"Huh?" Now the crowd was starting to think the painter was missing a few screws.

Zhang Sengyou, who lived during the Liang Dynasty, was revered for his lifelike paintings. Members of royalty and the nobility were so **enamoured** with his artwork that they would often commission him to paint pictures for them.

The monks of Anle Temple, too, admired his paintings so they asked him to paint four dragons on the walls surrounding the building. When word broke out that the master painter was in their town, the citizens rushed over to the temple to watch Zhang Sengyou at work. They saw him deep in focus, paying careful attention to every small detail of the artwork.

When it was completed, the dragons looked so majestic and vivacious that the crowd was stunned and **intimidated**. But one onlooker was puzzled by one small detail.

"Hey!" the old man said. "Why do none of the dragons have pupils in their eyes?" Everyone began looking closely at the mural. The crowd murmured, thinking that Zhang Sengyou had overlooked this.

"A dragon's spirit lies in the eyes," Zhang Sengyou replied. "Once I add the dots to complete the painting, the dragons will come to life and fly away."

That was the moment when the crowd fell about laughing. After people accused him of being a **lunatic**, Zhang Sengyou sighed heavily, picked up his paintbrush and added pupils to the eyes of two dragons.

Immediately, the sky turned dark, the wind wailed and created a flurry of fallen leaves, thunder boomed like fired cannons, and everyone got soaked from the heavy downpour of rain. Amidst this **hullabaloo**, the two dragons with the completed eyes popped out of the wall, soared up to the sky and disappeared.

The wind and rain abruptly ended and all that was left was a stunned, silent crowd and a smiling Zhang Sengyou.

Literal meaning

paint the dragon, dot the eyes

Figurative meaning

to add the final, important point to an artwork, piece of writing, etc.; to bring to life

Similar phrase in English

put the final/finishing touch

e.g. Let me just **put the final touch** to my artwork titled "Blocked Nose" by adding this used tissue I just sneezed into.

Learn about words

1. **enamoured** adj. : liking something a lot
2. **intimidated** adj. : being made afraid or nervous
3. **lunatic** n. : a mentally unstable person
4. **hullabaloo** n. : a loud disturbance or activity

Learn some phrases

1. missing a few screws

describes someone who is crazy or weird

e.g. Winnie is **missing a few screws**. She likes to collect her toenail clippings.

2. word breaks out

news, information or gossip that starts to spread among people

老馬識途
An old hand

"**M**y Lord. We have marched back to where we were this morning. We have still not left the **valley**."

Upon hearing this news, Duke Huan, who ruled during the Spring and Autumn Period, buried his head in his hands. He felt they might never get out of the valley and was starting to lose hope.

"Goodness grief!" the Duke exclaimed. "It's like we are going around in circles."

Accompanied by his trusted adviser, Prime Minister Guan Zhong, the Duke and his army were trying to return home to the state of Qi. His men had previously fought a victorious battle to drive out the northern **barbarian** tribes of Shanrong and Guzhu that had invaded Qi's ally, the state of Yan.

When the Duke and his troops first passed through the valley on their way up north, it was springtime. After they defeated the invaders and travelled back south, it was winter and the **landscape** had changed.

That same valley now looked totally different. **Scouts** were sent to find an exit but came back with no good news. Food was getting scarce and morale among the troops was falling day by day.

"Prime minister!" the Duke screamed in frustration. "If we don't get out of here we will never see our loved ones ever again. We're doomed, I tell you... doomed!" The duke felt he was trapped in that valley like a rat was trapped in a cage.

Luckily for him, Guan Zhong was an experienced official who stayed calm and thought long and hard about how to get home.

"My Lord," said the prime minister, "did you know that old horses remember the paths they have been on? Let's choose some old horses and see if they can lead us back to where we started."

"Really?" the Duke said, wondering if Guan Zhong had gone crazy after being stuck in the valley for days. He was, though, desperate to try anything to get out of that hell hole so he gave his prime minister the go ahead.

Guan Zhong immediately rounded up some old horses, released them and let them roam freely.

At first, they wandered around aimlessly, but then something strange happened: they all grouped together and moved in one direction.

"Follow those horses, men!" the Duke exclaimed. "They know the way home!"

Sure enough, those horses led the way out of the valley and found the main road back to Qi.

Literal meaning

old horses know the way

Figurative meaning

an experienced person knows what to do

Similar phrase in English

be an old hand at something

e.g. My grandfather is **an old hand at playing mahjong** and wins a lot every time he plays.

Learn about words

1. **valley** n. : low land area between mountains
2. **barbarian** n. : a person from a uncivilised, violent culture
3. **landscape** n. : large area of land especially whe referring to its appearance
4. **scout** n. : a soldier sent to gather information about the enemy, land, etc.

Learn some phrases

1. bury your face in your hands

   to cover your face with your hands because you are upset or disappointed

   e.g. Grandma Wong **buried her face in her hands** when Grandpa gave her an iron and an ironing board as a birthday present.

2. day by day

   more and more every day

   e.g. Cindy's disappointed grew **day by day** whenever she failed her exams.

害群之馬
A bad apple that spoils the bunch

The mythical Yellow Emperor had many qualities — wise, **virtuous**, inventive, to name but a few. But despite his magnificence, he could not prevent the one thing all travellers do when entering unknown territory: get lost.

The Yellow Emperor rode on a carriage to visit his dear old friend Dawei, who lived on Mount Juci located in an eastern region that is now Henan Province. His loyal men took an unfamiliar path and ended up going around in circles. Fortunately, a herdboy guiding a herd of horses passed by their carriage.

"Young lad!" the Yellow Emperor cried out. "Do you know the way to Mount Juci?"

"That I do," the herdboy said, and then he raised a finger, pointing to where they should go.

"And do you know where the gentleman Dawei lives?" the Yellow Emperor asked.

"That I do," the boy replied. The route to Dawei's home was so **convoluted** that an intellectual's brain would have exploded trying to make sense of it all, and yet the herdboy gave simple yet clear instructions on how to get to the man's **abode**.

"Great heavens!" the Yellow Emperor exclaimed. "How do you know that?" In response, the herdboy merely shrugged his shoulders.

"He may look like a simple herdboy," the Yellow Emperor thought to himself, "but he is actually a clever lad." He felt the urge to obtain greater insights into life.

"I have another question for you," the Yellow Emperor said. "This country has many problems. I want my people to be good, but some choose to be bad. What should I do?"

"Whatever you want to do," the boy said. "All I care about is freely wandering the land with my horses."

"Oh, come now!" the Yellow Emperor exclaimed. "You are wise beyond your years. Let's say you were in my position. What would you do?"

The herdboy did not have to think long as he already knew the answer: "Governing a country is no different from looking after horses. If you see a horse that is wild and has a bad influence on other horses, then you get rid of that horse. The same principle applies to ruling a country — cut out the cancer before it spreads to the entire nation."

The Yellow Emperor was **gobsmacked**. He bowed in gratitude, feeling much enlightened by the words of wisdom from a lowly herdboy.

Literal meaning

a horse that harms the herd

Figurative meaning

a person who harms the group or the community

Similar phrase in English

one bad apple spoils the bunch

> e.g. I fired Ming because he got his co-workers to call in sick and then spend the whole day at a theme park. He is **a bad apple that spoils the bunch**.

Learn about words

1. **virtuous** adj. : having high moral standards and good behaviour

2. **convoluted** adj. : complicated because of many twist and turns

3. **abode** n. : a house or home

4. **gobsmacked** adj. : describes you cannot speak because you are so surprised

Learn some phrases

1. wise beyond one's years

being a lot wiser and more intelligent than other people in your age group

> e.g. Betty is **wise beyond her years**. She is only 14 years old and she already has a savings plan so that she can retire at the age of 30.

2. cut out the cancer

to remove what is harmful, bad influence to a group, society, etc.

> e.g. Tony taught students swear words. We should **cut out the cancer** and fire him.

塞翁失馬
A blessing in disguise

A beautiful, black horse was slowly trotting with other horses on the ranch. His **gait** suddenly quickened to a **canter** and then he galloped at lightning speed, breaking free from the herd.

An old man watched the horse run away and go beyond the border to where the foreigners lived. He did not say a word or even raise an eyebrow; he just observed the loss of a horse like he was **impassively** watching the sun set in the evening.

He and his family were highly skilled at breeding horses, so to lose a valuable horse was big news in the community. All his neighbours paid him a visit to offer their condolences.

"This is such tragic news," one woman said. "You must feel so sad."

"Why should I be?" the old man replied. "Who knows? It might end up as a blessing." His neighbours thought the loss had made him slightly barmy.

Months later, that same horse came back with a group of fine horses raised by the foreign tribe. The neighbours once again came over but this time to congratulate him.

"You were right," a neighbour said. "You must feel so fortunate."

"Why should I be?" the old man replied while shrugging his shoulders. "Who knows? It might end up as bad luck." His neighbours shook their heads in disbelief.

Not long after, the old man's son rode one of the horses. The animal was still untamed and kept **bucking**, sending the lad into the air. He fell hard on the ground and broke his leg. It was feared he would not be able to walk properly again.

"Surely you must be upset now!" said a neighbour.

"Why should I be?" the old man replied without a hint of emotion.

"Your son is a cripple!"

"Who knows? It might turn out to be good luck," the old man replied. His neighbours believed he had definitely gone bonkers.

And yet Lady Luck did smile on the old man again. When the foreign warriors invaded the lands south of the border, the king ordered all able-bodied men from that region to take arms and repel the invaders. Parents wailed after they learnt that everyone's sons were killed in battle.

But not every young man had died; only the old man's son was alive. He never left home in the first place because he had a limp, and therefore told not to follow the other men to their doomed fate.

Literal meaning

an old man living at the frontier loses a horse

Figurative meaning

a misfortune may turn out to be good and vice versa

Similar phrase in English

a blessing in disguise

e.g. Being late for the singing contest was **a blessing in disguise** because there was a small fire at the contest hall.

Learn about words

1. **gait** n. : a certain style of walking or running
2. **canter** v. : a horse running quite fast but in an easy and relaxed way
3. **impassively** adv. : doing something that has no emotion or reaction
4. **buck** v. : a horse kicking the back legs into the air

Learn some phrases

1. **go bonkers**

to be silly or crazy

e.g. Jane **went bonkers** and said she wanted to be a cat for the rest of her life.

2. **Lady Luck smiles on someone**

saying someone is lucky or has luck

e.g. **Lady Luck has smiled on me** today. I won the first prize in the lucky draw - Maths books worth over $5,000!

歧路亡羊
Straying from the right path

Yangzi, a scholar who lived during the Warring States Period, was at home and deep in thought when he suddenly heard Bang! Bang! He got up and opened the front door to reveal his **frantic** looking neighbour.

"Sir!" his neighbour cried out. "Please help me find a lost sheep. My family, friends and relatives are already helping me look for the animal!"

Yangzi arched an eyebrow and asked: "All these people looking for one sheep?"

"Yes! It is not as simple as it sounds. There is a **fork** in the road so we need people to explore all possible routes. Trust me. Time is of the essence!"

The renowned thinker pitied the man and felt it was his duty to help. He called for his servant and told him to join the search.

After many hours, most members of the search party had returned to the village looking tired and frustrated.

Yangzi spotted his neighbour and asked: "Any luck?"

"None, whatsoever," his downcast neighbour replied while shaking his head. "Each fork in the main road led to more forks and so on. There are so many possible routes the sheep could have chosen.

"There was just no point in continuing or else we

would have all got lost ourselves!"

Yangzi **pondered** deeply on what his neighbour said. Lines started to form on his forehead and then he sighed as if the world weighed on his shoulders.

Mengsun Yang, his student, saw his teacher remain quiet for some time.

"Sir! Why are you so upset? The sheep is not valuable and is not even yours."

"I have learnt something here," said the scholar. "The great path is lost because there are too many forks."

"Huh? Come again?" Mengsun Yang thought his teacher was talking in a foreign language.

Yangzi finally smiled at his student's **naive** way of thinking.

"If we fail to choose the correct road, we will wind up like these confused people looking for one lost sheep. Therefore, we must find the right direction in life and not lose focus, or else we will risk losing everything and there will be no way back."

Literal meaning

lost sheep on a forked road

Figurative meaning

complex situation or thoughts can lead to confusion, making people fail to achieve their goal in the end

Similar phrase in English

to stray from the right path

[e.g.] Ah Fai had to make sure his son **did not stray from the right path** after the boy said his dream was to be a super villain.

Learn about words

1. frantic **adj.** : very upset because of fear or worry
2. fork **n.** : where a road or river divides into two parts
3. ponder **v.** : to think carefully for a period of time
4. naive **adj.** : lack of knowledge or life experience; too willing to believe people

Learn some phrases

1. time is of the essence

    said to encourage someone to speed up

    [e.g.] We have one day to bake a hundred pies. **Time is of the essence!**

2. wind up

    to find yourself in an unwanted situation because of something you did

    [e.g.] He **wound up** being obese after eating ten burgers a day for a whole year.

亡羊補牢

Better late than never

Zhuang Xin, a loyal minister from the state of Chu, was supposed to show respect in front of his king. Instead, he paced the court from side to side, waving his arms.

"Your Majesty," he said to King Xiang, "you are often surrounded by Duke Zhou, Duke Xia, Lord Yanling, and Lord Shouling. May I speak plainly: they are frivolous playboys and only interested in living a life of leisure."

"Get to the point!" the king said, feeling a bit testy.

"The point is these pointless people are stopping you from noticing what your enemies are up to," Zhang Xin replied, "and that could lead to Chu's downfall."

"You are **deluded**," said King Xiang. "Chu is not at war with its neighbours. Where's the risk?"

"It's all an illusion, Your Highness. Chu's rivals are waiting for the right moment to attack."

The king's face went purple with rage. "How dare you speak ill of your country!"

Zhuang Xin felt sad by the king's reply. "If Your Majesty does not believe me, please allow me to live in the state of Zhao for some time and see how events unfold." The king agreed to this request. He could not wait to see the back of Zhuang Xin.

Five months later, the Qin army invaded Chu and took most of the land and the major cities, including the capital. King Xiang had to leave his palace and go into exile. He then remembered Zhuang Xin's advice and felt like an idiot for not listening to him. The king sent soldiers to bring his former minister to appear before him.

"My dear Zhuang Xin," greeted the **ashamed** King Xiang, "I've been a pigheaded fool and should have listened to you. Am I too late to fix the problem?"

Zhuang Xin's face lit up with hope and said: "Let me tell you a story, Your Excellency. A shepherd found a hole in the **sheepfold** but did not repair it. A few days later, several sheep went missing. His friend told him it was not too late to **mend** the sheepfold. That is what the shepherd did and he never lost sheep again.

"It's not too late to mend your 'sheepfold', Your Majesty. As long as you are determined to revive the state, it is not an impossible task!"

King Xiang nodded to show he understood the moral of the story. With Zhuang Xin's help, the king was able to revitalise the state and recapture lost territories.

Literal meaning

mend the sheepfold after the sheep escaped

Figurative meaning

correct mistakes even after a problem has occurred

Similar phrase in English

better late than never

e.g. So you finally decided to apologise to your brother after you stole his milkshake 40 years ago. Oh well, **better late than never**.

Learn about words

1. deluded **adj.** : believing in something that is not true
2. ashamed **adj.** : feeling guilty about what you have done
3. sheepfold **n.** : a sheep pen
4. mend **v.** : to repair

Learn some phrases

1. get to the point

   to express the crucial part of something written or said

   e.g. You spent two hours talking about healthy habits. Just get to the point and say eat well, do regular exercise and sleep early.

2. speak ill of someone/something

   to say something harmful or unkind about someone/something

   e.g. Ah Mei spoke ill of me and now my reputation is ruined.

聞雞起舞
Strike while the iron is hot

Cock-a-doodle-do! Zu Ti was awakened by the sound of the rooster heralding the break of **dawn** and the time to get your day started. But as soon as he opened his eyes, he knew immediately something was wrong.

He turned and looked at Liu Tun with whom he shared a bed with. His best friend was still snoring and in a deep slumber, so Zu Ti kicked him in the leg.

"Huh?" A groggy Liu Tun responded.

"Wake up!" Zu Ti hollered. "Did you hear that? That is so strange."

They both remained quiet while the rooster **crowed** once again.

"Nothing strange with that," Liu Tun said while his eyes were still closed. "The rooster does that every morning."

"But it's not the morning," Zu Ti said. "It's the middle of the night and the moon is so bright."

Liu Tun sat up straight away. He was wide awake now.

"That has never happened before," Liu Tun said, feeling uneasy now. "It's a bad omen and could signify danger."

Both men were government officials in Sizhou during the Western Jin Dynasty. It was a dark time when northern tribes kept invading the country, and various conflicts and power struggles dominated the royal court. The two friends shared common ideals and spent many nights discussing how to resolve external threats and revive the country.

"It is not a bad omen," Zu Ti replied, "but a wake-up call to be **proactive**! Let's get up and practise martial arts every time we hear the rooster crow."

Without delay, they got out of bed, got dressed, and practised fighting with swords under the moonlit night sky. Every night, the sound of the rooster was later followed by the clashing of swords until the first light of dawn. They trained like this for a long time and became expert swordsmen.

Years later, both men served their country as generals, leading armies to victories against invaders and reclaiming territories that were previously lost to the barbarians from the north.

None of this would have happened if they had just stayed in bed, like many of us would, and kept talking about how to save the country when what was required was immediate action on **cultivating** themselves.

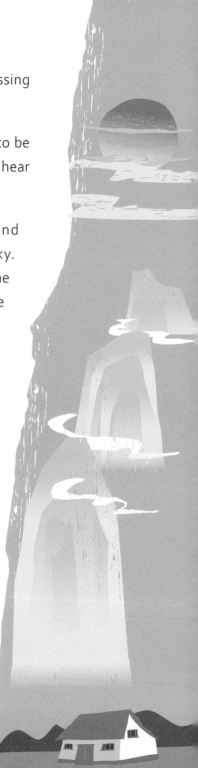

Literal meaning

dance with a sword when you hear the rooster crow

Figurative meaning

be motivated and ready to take advantage of opportunities

Similar phrase in English

strike while the iron is hot

e.g. I've never seen Ah Gong study so hard. We need to **strike while the iron is hot** and study with him.

Learn about words

1. dawn **n.** : the first light in the sky before the sun rises
2. crow **v.** : a rooster makes a long, loud and sharp sound
3. proactive **adj.** : taking action to make a change rather than waiting
4. cultivate **v.** : to develop or improve something through education

Learn some phrases

1. deep slumber

   heavy sleep

   e.g. Ah Mei has gone into a **deep slumber**. She must be very tired.

2. bad omen

   a sign that something bad will happen in the future

   e.g. You dropped the egg! That is a **bad omen**! The world will be destroyed by a nuclear war in three days!

呆若木雞
At a loss for words

"Why is it that we spent a lot of time and money on these roosters and yet they win some fights and then lose the next one? I want an undefeated champion!"

The King of Qi was peeved; he demanded an answer from his eunuchs. None of them had an answer for him.

Earlier, the king had watched one of his roosters do battle in his weekly cockfighting sessions, but his bird lost to a smaller opponent.

"Your Majesty," one eunuch piped up, "I know of a man named Ji Xian who is an expert cockfight trainer. He will definitely turn one rooster into a champion." The king immediately sent a servant to bring Ji Xian to the palace.

When Ji Xian arrived at the court, the king told him: "I want you to train a rooster so that it can win cockfights immediately."

"It will take time to train a champion, Your Majesty," Ji Xian said. The king did not want to hear that but had to follow his advice.

Ji Xian selected a promising rooster from the flock and locked himself in a room. Ten days passed and the king was getting **restless**, so he ordered a eunuch to find out why Ji Xian was taking so long.

"Is the rooster ready?" the eunuch asked.

"No," Ji Xian replied, "he's still proud and gets angry easily."

Another ten days passed and the king was getting impatient. He sent a eunuch to demand why Ji Xian had not brought the rooster out.

"He is still not calm," Ji Xian replied. "The bird reacts easily to sounds and **stimulating** objects."

Ten more days passed, and the king had finally had enough. He summoned Ji Xian to appear before him.

"This rooster is too **aggressive** and has an angry look," explained Ji Xian.

"Then he is brave!" the king said.

Ji Xian shook his head. "You have raised many brave roosters. Are they champions?" The king did not reply, and was irritated the trainer was a smart alec. The king decided to not bother Ji Xian anymore but after ten days had passed, the trainer brought the rooster to the court.

"He's ready!" Ji Xian said. "He no longer reacts to other roosters crowing. He is so **unflappable** that he looks like a wooden chicken. Other roosters will be fearful of such a cool, calm, and collected opponent."

"Finally!" the king exclaimed. The rooster did not disappoint the king as he went on to win countless

Literal meaning

expressionless like a wooden chicken

Figurative meaning

originally meant as being calm and having self-control, but now is used to describe being stunned and speechless

Similar phrase in English

at a loss for words

e.g. When I saw our PE teacher Mr Chan wearing a broccoli costume, I was **at a loss for words**.

Learn about words

1. **restless** adj. : unable to relax or stay still
2. **stimulating** adj. : causing interest and enthusiasm
3. **aggressive** adj. : being angry and wanting to attack others
4. **unflappable** adj. : showing calmness and self-control

Learn some phrases

1. smart alec

   someone who gives answers in a clever way that is very annoying

   e.g. I realised that Ah Hung was a smart alec when I asked her what the time was and she said it was time I bought a watch.

2. cool, calm, and collected

   describes being able to control one's emotions

   e.g. Eric was cool, calm, and collected during such a stressful situation.

螳 臂 當 車
An inflated sense of self

Butch the mantis was **stationed** at a checkpoint on a road leading to the woods when he saw a beetle approaching him.

"Halt! Who are you and why are you on this road?"

Butch gave Bertie Beetle a long, hard stare. The mantis stood upright and crossed his huge **forelegs** as if he were ready for a fight. He was given strict instructions by the Mantis King not to let anyone enter the woods as his highness was taking a nap.

"I-I'm on m-my way to visit my s-sick and p-poor mother on the other side of the w-woods," Bertie said.

"Not on this road," Butch said. "Turn around and take another one." Bertie sighed, turned back, and went the long way around.

Also travelling on that same road was a carriage carrying the Duke; he was heading to the woods to go hunting with his men. The Duke had excellent eyesight and saw something up ahead on the road that looked a bit odd.

As the carriage moved closer to the stationary mantis, the Duke saw that the green insect was standing up with his forelegs spread outwards as if it was ready to push something heavy.

The carriage got closer and closer to the mantis. Still, Butch would not move. The brave yet foolish insect was going to stay on that spot even when faced with death.

"Stop!" the Duke ordered the driver. The carriage screeched to a halt in front of the mantis.

"What's that insect?" he asked his driver. "It **has guts to** risk being **crushed** to death."

"It's a mantis, My Lord. Its forelegs are so strong it can grip much larger animals, such as frogs, so that they cannot escape, and then it will eat its prey."

"Incredible!" the Duke exclaimed. "It thinks it has super strength. I do believe when it saw the carriage, it wanted to stop us and push us away. If this mantis were a man, it'd be the bravest soldier ever."

The duke gave a **hearty laugh** and then ordered: "Turn the carriage around! The road is blocked by this insect!"

The carriage backed away from Butch, who stood firm and **erect**, and travelled back in the same direction it came from.

With a triumphant glow on his face, Butch declared: "Only a fool would dare to get past me!"

Literal meaning

a mantis tries to stop a carriage

Figurative meaning

to overrate yourself and attempt something impossible

Similar phrase in English

inflated sense of self

e.g. Ricky Wu has such an **inflated sense of self** after he found out he shared the same birthday as Albert Einstein.

Learn about words

1. station **v.** : to be at a place to do a job
2. foreleg **n.** : front leg
3. crush **v.** : destroy something by pressing on it hard
4. erect **adj.** : standing upright

Learn some phrases

1. have guts to

   to be brave and determined.

   e.g. Firefighters **have guts to** enter buildings that are on fire.

2. hearty laugh

   a strong, unrestrained and warm laugh

   e.g. Becky gave a **hearty laugh** when she saw her dad split the seat of his trousers when he sat down.

井 底 之 蛙
Broaden your horizons

Boing... splish, boing... splash, boing... splosh! Jumping on pools of water is fun when you are a child, but you eventually grow up and find other ways to amuse yourself. But for one particular frog, he had been doing it for years.

"Ah... **This is the life**," Freddie the frog said after he spent a few minutes manically jumping around the bottom of the well.

"Life does not get any better than this!" He sat back near the side of the well and looked around his home with a self-satisfied grin spread across his face. He had lived at the bottom of the well all his life so he had no experience of anything else apart from that cramped, wet, dark hole.

One day, the frog jumped up to the edge at the top of the well. Blue skies were above, while a gentle breeze ruffled the grass below him. Freddie, as usual, was unaware of the beauty of his surroundings.

He was just about to turn and jump back down to his beloved home when, **from the corner of his eye**, he saw Toby the turtle passing by. He had just come back from a journey across the ocean where he saw many incredible sights.

Upon seeing Toby, Freddie could not help but think what a sorry creature the turtle was and how empty his life must be. "Hey, Turtle! Look at me!" Freddie did a little **jig** to show how happy he was.

"You do seem pleased with yourself," Toby said. "Go on, tell me why."

"I live in the best place in the world. I can hop around the edge of the well. I can splash about in the water. When I am tired, I can take a rest at the side. If I want to have some really crazy fun, I can jump in the mud and make funny squelching noises. Why don't you join me? Every day is a holiday here!"

Freddie's great love for the well had made Toby **curious**, so he looked down. All he saw was still water in a dark hole.

"Goodness gracious!" cried the turtle. He jumped away from the well like he just had an electric shock.

"Hey, Froggy. Do you know how wide and deep it is?"

"No and no," replied Freddie. "Who cares when I have my well?"

"Let me open your eyes," Toby said. "The ocean is so wide it takes me many days to cross it. It is so deep that I have never swum to the bottom. It is so big that floods and **droughts** do not affect it. Your well gets flooded during heavy rain and has no water during a drought. Am I right?"

Freddie did not say anything.

Toby continued: "The ocean is where you see a wide variety of marine life of all sizes, from **enormous** whales to tiny seahorses."

"Bye, and have fun by yourself in your little well!"

Literal meaning

the frog at the bottom of the well

Figurative meaning

a person of limited outlook and experience

Similar phrase in English

parochial mentality

having a view of life that is narrow and focused on their local area

[e.g.] Bobby has such a **parochial mentality**; he thinks Hong Kong culture is the best in the world despite not ever once leaving the city.

Learn about words

1. jig **n.** : a lively, jumping dance

2. curious **adj.** : eager to learn things

3. drought **n.** : no rain for a long time

4. enormous **adj.** : very big

Learn some phrases

1. this is the life

a saying to express you are enjoying something in your life

[e.g.] This is the life. I just love taking a relaxing bath while watching Korean dramas and eating a hamburger and French fries.

2. from the corner of one's eye

to see something but not clearly because you did not look at it directly

[e.g.] From the corner of his eye, Tony saw rats enter the restaurant's kitchen.

鷸 蚌 相 爭
Profiting from a stalemate

"Hey, move it you softies, or else I'll crack your shells! This is my place." Clint the clam kicked some sand at some other clams who had foolishly laid in the spot where he normally stayed. The nervous clams quickly **shuffled** away.

This cocky clam had a strong shell and that made him think he was a tough, little **mollusc**. Afraid of nothing, he opened his shell up wide so that he could feel the warmth of the sun's rays.

Circling high above in the sky, Snoopy the snipe saw the clam had exposed himself.

"A-ha!" Snoopy cried. "Dinner is served!"

The snipe swooped down on his prey to snatch the juicy flesh inside the shell. Out of the corner of his eye, Clint spotted the snipe the moment the bird was just a few centimetres away from him.

SNAP! Like a mousetrap snaring a **rodent**, the clam shut his shells and trapped the snipe's bill.

"Ouch!" Snoopy screamed.

The snipe dragged the clam along the ground with his bill, but he could not get rid of Clint. He tried a different tactic.

"Hey there. Why don't you open up and let me go? I promise not to eat you!"

"Yeah, sure," the clam said, "and pigs might fly too!"

The snipe stopped pretending to be nice.

"Listen up, tough guy," Snoopy hissed, "you had better open up or you will die of thirst. There will be no rain for days and you are far from the shore so the tide won't reach you."

The clam argued back: "Did you think I was born yesterday? You will die of hunger too if you cannot get any food."

Snoopy tried to shake off the clam but Clint hung onto him as if he had been superglued to the snipe's beak.

Fisherman Fu was walking along the beach on his way home when he saw this **tussle**. He could see that each side was locked in a battle neither one could win.

"Ha, what a lucky day," he thought. He sneaked up to the warring pair and simply picked them both up with his net. He continued his journey back home, thinking about the different ways his wife could cook the snipe and clam for their meal that night.

Literal meaning

the clam and the snipe locked in combat

Figurative meaning

two sides who cannot agree lose out to a third party

Similar phrase in English

two dogs fight for a bone, while a third runs away with it

e.g. I saw **two dogs fight for a bone, while a third runs away with it.**
Two housewives were arguing over who should sit in the empty
seat but did not notice a young boy had sneaked over and sat in

Learn about words

1. shuffle **v.** : to move your feet without lifting them off the ground

2. mollusc **n.** : a creature with a soft body, no spine and often covered in a shell

3. rodent **n.** : a small mammal with sharp, front teeth, such as mice

4. tussle **n.** : to wrestle in a fight in a very strong way

Learn some phrases

1. pigs might fly

saying you think there is no chance of something happening

e.g. Meghan says she will marry a prince one day. **Pigs might fly**, too.

2. Did you think I was born yesterday?

saying you are not stupid or easily fooled

e.g. I know you are secretly recording our conversation with your phone.
Did you think I was born yesterday?

沉魚落雁
Drop-dead gorgeous

In ancient China, four women were famous for being beautiful: Xishi, Wang Zhaojun, Diaochan and Yang Yuhuan. These divine ladies were known to make kings or generals go weak at the knees; some of them were criticised for **bewitching** kings, making them forget about running their kingdoms.

Animals were also not **immune** to their loveliness. When Xishi washed clothes in a nearby river, the fish were so entranced that they would feel ashamed of their looks compared to that heavenly image above them and then they would sink to the bottom of the river.

Wang Zhaojun was another beauty who could stop anyone dead in their tracks. She lived during a time when the emperor was fearful of the Xiongnu, a northern tribe that kept invading China. The emperor did not want a war with the Xiongnu so he asked his adviser on how to prevent this. His adviser suggested that one of the palace ladies marrying their ruler.

The emperor did not want one of his beauties given to a barbarian. "Who is the ugliest one in the palace?" he asked.

All the paintings of the palace women were displayed in front of the emperor at court. He thought all the pictures were of beautiful women apart from one.

"This plain-looking, gap-toothed girl with the big **mole** on her upper lip is perfect!" the emperor said when he saw Wang Zhaojun's portrait. But the truth was that the court painter had not received a **bribe** from Wang Zhaojun so he painted her with an ugly face.

Just before Wang Zhaojun left to go north, the emperor got to see the lovely lady for the first time.

"Oh my God!" the emperor yelled. "That's not the girl I saw in the picture. Send another one instead!"

"I'm sorry Your Majesty," his adviser said, "but we already made a promise to the Xiongnu to send this one." The emperor reluctantly let Wang Zhaojun leave and then ordered his court painter to be executed.

When geese flying in the sky saw Wang Zhaojun travelling north, they were so stunned by her beauty that they forgot to flap their wings, fell to the ground and died.

Just like Xishi, Wang Zhaojun had the power to bring anyone down all because they were blessed with a prettiness that was unreal.

Literal meaning

fish sinking, geese falling

Figurative meaning

to describe a very beautiful woman

Similar phrase in English

drop-dead gorgeous

e.g. Let's ask Tommy if we can go to his flat to do our school project. His older sister will be there, too. She is **drop-dead gorgeous!**

Learn about words

1. bewitch **v.** : to attract and have power over someone
2. immune **adj.** : not affected by something
3. mole **n.** : a small, dark spot on the skin
4. bribe **n.** : illegal money or gift to someone for a favour

Learn some phrases

1. weak at the knees

   to lose stability when with someone you are attracted to

   e.g. Ivy went weak at the knees when Handsome Henry said "Hello" and told her she had some rice on her face.

2. stop dead in your tracks

   to suddenly stop moving or doing something

   e.g. When I saw 100 cockroaches, I stopped dead in my tracks.

狼狽為奸
Good teamwork to achieve wicked goals

illy the Bei and Willy the Wolf were out and about one early morning in search of some juicy animals they could sink their teeth into for breakfast.

The Bei was a mythical creature that lived near the Changbai Mountain in Northeast Asia between China and northern Korea. Just like the unicorn, the Bei has never been seen before, but it was said to be similar to a wolf but with longer legs. These two crafty animals were good pals and they often worked together to hunt sheep and cows.

The **devious** duo wandered around a mountain until they saw a sheep pen down below. There were enough sheep for them to have breakfast, lunch, and dinner for many days. Their mouths started to **water** when they saw **dozens** of fattened sheep hemmed in on all four sides. The problem was that the sheepfold was made of four high walls and the gate was locked.

"There is no way we can jump over the wall," Billy said. "Let's try climbing over it."

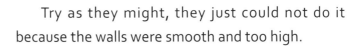

Try as they might, they just could not do it because the walls were smooth and too high.

Willy then took ten steps back and ran at top speed to ram a hole in the wall.

BANG!

"Ouch!" cried Willy, holding his head where a bruise was forming. Despite the pain, he did not

want to give up as the sound of the sheep bleating on the other side of the wall made him crazy for some lamb chops.

"We need to use what is inside our heads," Willy said, regretting his ill-thought attempt at **penetrating** the wall.

"Why don't you stand on my shoulders to climb over first?" Billy said. "My hind legs are much longer and I can stand on my toes to make myself taller and push you up higher."

Willy clambered up on Billy's shoulder and was finally able to raise himself up to the top. The wolf then pulled up his partner in crime. They both sat on the top, legs dangling over the wall and eyes wide open. They felt they were about to drop into paradise.

The sheep looked up and started panicking, bleating and running over to the other side. Some of them tried to climb the wall but they were not as clever as the tricky twosome.

"Those silly sheep don't know anything about teamwork," the Bei said.

"Lucky for us, you mean," the wolf replied. "Bon appétit, my good friend!"

Literal meaning

a wolf and a bei work together to do something bad

Figurative meaning

to work well together for a wicked purpose

Similar phrase in English

in cahoots (with)

> e.g. Jinny was **in cahoots with** Terry. They tried to cheat in the test but were caught by Mr Wong.

Learn about words

1. **devious** adj. : behaving in a dishonest or tricky way to get something
2. **water** v. : the smell or sight of food makes you produces saliva
3. **dozen** n. : a group of 12
4. **penetrate** v. : to go into or through something

Learn some phrases

1. hem in

   to surround someone closely

   > e.g. I was **hemmed in** by a bunch of speaking potatos in a dream.

2. bon appetit

   to sag before a meal to wish people to enjoy the food

   > e.g. This dish is my special recipe of spicy, fried cow ears. **Bon appetit!**

黔驢技窮
A one-trick donkey

"EE-AW! EE-AW! EE-AW!" A fed-up and hungry donkey had been walking for many days it just could not hide its displeasure.

"Sh-Shush! Hic! Ss-stop your **braying**... Hic!"

Johnny the trader had been leading that donkey for a long time in a dark forest in Qian, which is now Guizhou Province. Along the way, he had drunk far too many bottles of wine. He had no idea where he was going.

"I'm going to use the toilet behind those bushes," he told the donkey. "Don't get into trouble while I'm gone."

He tied this **beast of burden** to a tree and then stumbled away to find a nice spot to empty his bladder. He tried to make his way back to the donkey, but forgot where he tied the animal. The donkey was all on his own now and could not go far.

The animals in Qian had never seen a donkey before. It looked really strange to them and they were not sure if it was friendly or not. Terry the tiger was out looking for food when he saw the donkey.

"Yikes! What is that thing with big muscles on its backside and teeth too big for its mouth?" Terry hid behind a tree to **spy** on the animal from a safe place.

"Ee-aw! Ee-aw!" The donkey's braying made the tiger run away like a frightened pussycat.

Day after day, the tiger watched the donkey from a distance. All Terry saw was the donkey doing nothing except making that terrible noise.

After a while, Terry got used to the braying and became less afraid of it. He decided to walk over to the animal again. This time the tiger got a proper look at the donkey up close.

"You don't look that scary at all," Terry said. "Silly me, I must get my eyes checked one of these days."

Now feeling confident, Terry bumped into the donkey.

"Oi! Who do you think you are? You **clumsy** oaf?" the donkey yelled. It gave the tiger a big kick with its **hind** legs. Terry hardly felt anything.

"A-ha! So that's it! You can only bray and kick," said the tiger while licking his wet lips.

Terry immediately jumped on top of the donkey. The poor creature kept braying but it did not take long for the hungry tiger to stop that sound once and for all.

Literal meaning

the donkey in Qian has used up its tricks

Figurative meaning

describes someone who has used up his or her limited abilities to overcome a challenge

Similar phrase in English

a one-trick pony

> [e.g.] That film critic Jim Bogmarsh only knows about movies and nothing else. What **a one-trick pony**!

Learn about words

1. braying [n.] : a loud noise a donkey or mule makes
2. spy [v.] : look at secretly
3. clumsy [adj.] : not smooth or careful when moving
4. hind [adj.] : at the back of an animal's body

Learn some phrases

1. beast of burden

an animal that pulls heavy things or carries heavy loads

> [e.g.] My Lord, our donkey is strong but you really cannot expect this **beast of burden** to carry your grand piano up the hill to your new castle.

2. once and for all

something done completely and finally

> [e.g.] This message proves **once and for all** you had been texting Sarah!

盲人摸象
Can't see the wood from the trees

In a remote village, eight men who were born blind were discussing what an elephant must be like as they had never encountered one before.

"An elephant must be a terrifying beast," said one blind man. "I heard it has two sharp horns. It also makes a **blood-curdling** trumpet sound."

"No, no, no!" said another blind man. "It's a gentle creature. They say the princess rides on its back at a very slow pace."

And so on and so on.

For days they kept arguing back and forth until they decided to settle it once and for all. The four blind men were led to the king's palace and were presented before the **sovereign**.

"Your Excellency," began a member of the blind man group, "we only hear about the outside world from the villagers. We humbly request to touch one of your elephants to understand what this magnificent creature is like."

The king was curious as to how each man would define an elephant. He told his ministers to take the men to the courtyard where an elephant would be waiting for them. When they got to the courtyard, the men's hands were placed on different parts of the elephant.

The man who touched the elephant's belly exclaimed, "A-ha! The creature is a giant pot!"

"What are you talking about?" said the man touching one of the **tusks**. "It is a long radish!"

"No way!" said the man touching an ear. "It is a winnowing basket."

"You're having a laugh!" said the man touching the trunk. "I can tell you for certain it is a huge **pestle**."

"Well, I'm certain that it is a pillar," said the man touching the leg.

Another was touching the back and said: "An elephant is most definitely a bed."

"You are one hundred percent wrong," said the man touching the tip of the tail. "It's a brush."

The man touching the elephant's head said: "I'm absolutely correct in saying that it is a huge stone."

Each man was so sure of what an elephant really was that they kept arguing for hours and could have done so until the cows came home.

Literal meaning

blind men touching an elephant

Figurative meaning

having a limited view because you do not see the whole picture

Similar phrase in English

can't see the wood from the trees

> [e.g.] Ah Mei spent hours checking on grammar mistakes but didn't reorganise her confusing essay. She **couldn't see the wood from the trees.**

Learn about words

1. **blood-curdling** [adj.] : describes something very frightening
2. **sovereign** [n.] : a king or a queen
3. **tusk** [n.] : the long, pointed teeth of an elephant or walrus
4. **pestle** [n.] : heavy stick made of stone for crushing herbs and spices

Learn some phrases

1. back and forth

   to be on side then be on the opposite side and then back again
   > [e.g.] Ah Ping and Ah Wai argued back and forth about which style was more effective: White Eyebrow Kung Fu or Drunken Monkey Fist.

2. until the cows come home

   for a long period of time
   > [e.g.] You can argue until the cows come home but I have made my decision.

Index

THE MAGIC FOUR 1

Written by Catherine Chan & Simon Lau
Illustrated by William Ma

Editor   Jamie Poon
Designer   M.M.Mak
Layout   Yanping Lai

Publisher
Chung Hwa Educational Services Company

Telephone   (852)2137 2338
Fax   (852)2713 8202
Email   info@chunghwabook.com.hk
Website   https://www.chunghwabook.com.hk

Distributer
SUP Publishing Logistics (HK) Limited
16/F, Tsuen Wan Industrial Centre, 220-248 Texaco Road, Tsuen Wan, NT, Hong Kong
Telephone   (852) 2150 2100
Fax   (852) 2407 3062
Email   info@suplogistics.com.hk

Printer
Elegance Printing & Book Binding Co., Ltd.
Block A, 4/F, Hoi Bun Industrial Bldg., 6 Wing Yip St., Kwun Tong, H.K.

ISBN 978-988-8861-52-1
First Edition, July 2024.
© Chung Hwa Educational Services Company

Details   210 x 190 mm